My First Illustrated Bible Story

The Empty Tomb

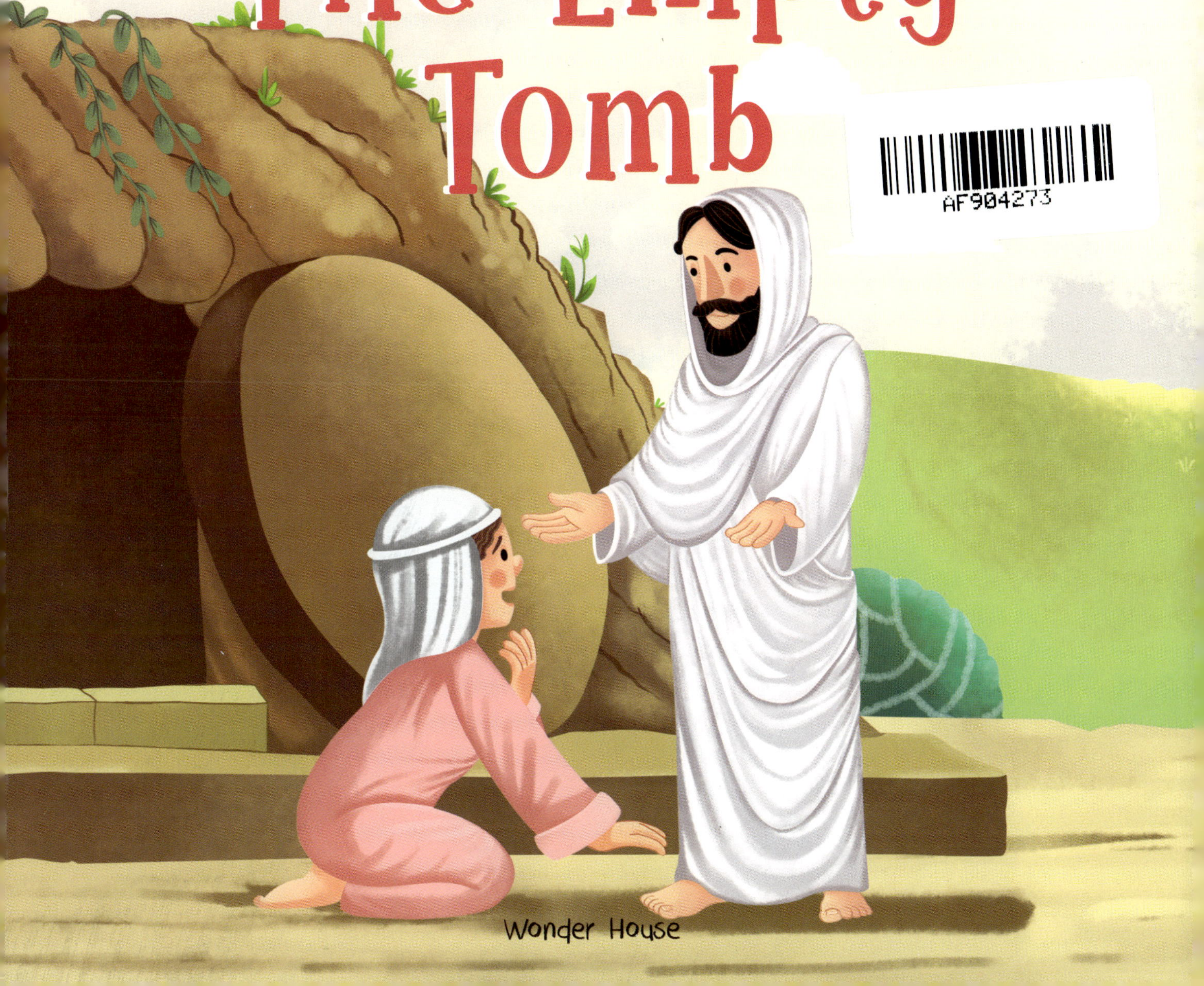

Wonder House

It was an early Sunday morning, two days after the death and burial of Jesus. Mary, along with a few women were going to visit Jesus's tomb.

When they reached the cave, they saw that the stone covering the cave's mouth had been rolled away and the guards were gone, the tomb of Jesus had been opened! The women were horrified. Little did they know that angels had rolled away the stone and the scared soldiers had run away.

'They did not even leave the Lord's body in peace,' cried Mary. The women ran back to the disciples to inform them what they had just witnessed.

Mary soon found Peter and John and told them in a frantic voice, 'They have taken away the Lord out of the tomb. I do not know where they have laid him!'

Peter and John were horrified as they rushed toward the tomb. They stood outside the cave for a moment. John went inside and Peter followed him. Seeing that Jesus's clothes and napkin had been carefully folded and kept over the casket, John realized, 'Jesus has risen from the dead!'

John believed that Jesus was alive. Both Peter and John went away, rejoicing. Soon, Mary returned to the tomb and wept thinking of her Lord. As she looked inside the cave, she saw two men in white garments on either side where the body of Jesus was laid. One of them asked her, 'Woman, why do you weep?' 'They have taken away my Lord,' cried Mary.

Suddenly, she heard a voice call her from behind, 'Mary!' At once, she knew that it was Jesus. She fell at his feet and cried, 'My Lord!'

Jesus calmed her and said, 'I am not yet going away to my Father. But go to my brothers, and say to them,' I go up to my Father and to your Father.' Mary ran, at once, to tell the disciples that she had indeed seen the Lord. This was the first time anyone had seen Jesus after he had risen from the dead.

Over the next few days, Jesus was seen by his disciples and his believers unexpectedly and briefly. This renewed their faith in him and as time passed, Jesus's disciples spread his teachings far and wide. His resurrection removed any doubts that people had in him.